The Wonderful World of Disney

THE ARISTOCATS

DERRYDALE BOOKS
New York

Madame Adelaide Bonfamille lived in Paris at the turn of the century. She had no children, but she had her four cats.

Duchess was a beautiful white cat, and her three kittens, Berlioz, Toulouse, and Marie were adorable balls of fur. They loved Madame very much, too, because she was a very kind old woman. She let them play about the house and even Roquefort the mouse was welcome in her home.

When the kittens were not playing, they pursued their talents. Toulouse was already an excellent artist. Madame had bought him an easel, a palette and lots of brushes and tubes of paint.

But Toulouse often preferred to paint
with his paws. He had a lot more fun
that way, splashing paint on the canvas.

Berlioz wanted to become a virtuoso pianist, while Marie dreamed of being an opera singer. Whenever Berlioz played the piano, she would sing along practicing her scales.

Inevitably, Toulouse would join them, and the kittens would break into a chorus. Berlioz would become the conductor, and they'd all end up laughing.

Roquefort and Madame always enjoyed the show and clapped loudly.

Their mother Duchess was very proud of them. Every day she told her kittens, "When you are famous one day, you must never forget to thank Madame Bonfamille! Without her help and support, you wouldn't go far. So always be grateful to her. She's done everything for us."

Little did Duchess know how much more Madame Bonfamille wanted to do for her cats.

Just that morning, the kind old lady had called her attorney, Mr Georges Hautecourt. She wanted to make a will and leave her estate and fortune to her cats. Mr Hautecourt drove to her home immediately. He had known Madame for many years and was very taken with her.

Poor Mr Hautecourt was very nearsighted. In greeting, he kissed Duchess's fluffy tail instead of Madame's hand. Madame giggled. Then Berlioz put on a waltz and Mr Hautecourt and Madame went twirling across the room.

Down in his room, Edgar the butler carefully listened through a pipe to their every move.

"My dear, dear Mr Hautecourt," he overheard Madame tell her friend when the waltz was over, "I called you for a very special reason. I have decided to leave my estate and fortune to my darling cats! I would like you to draw the will!"

Edgar was shocked. "How could she forget me after all I've done for her!" he grumbled. "There is only one way out of this: those cats must go!"

Edgar hurried to the kitchen. He had an idea. He added a few sleeping pills to the cats' dinner.

"Dinner's ready!" he called to the cats, who came running. They were very hungry because they had played all day long. They quickly lapped up their milk.

"I'm tired!" yawned Berlioz when he was done.

"Me too...." echoed Marie and Toulouse. Duchess was sleepy, as well. She took the kittens to their basket in Madame's room, and soon they were sound asleep.

When Madame was asleep as well, Edgar tiptoed into her room and stole the cats in their basket. He slipped out of the house. Without making a sound, he placed the basket in the sidecar of his motorcycle...

16

...and took off. He looked over his shoulder to make sure no one had seen him and ended bouncing down the stairs to the subway station!

When he got back out on the street,
Edgar headed for the countryside, where
he knew a river ran.

Edgar planned to leave the cats by the water. He grinned with anticipation as he imagined the looks on their faces the following morning. He was so wrapped up in his thoughts that he did not notice the two farm dogs by the side of the road. The roar of his motorcycle had alerted them and they were looking forward to a good chase.

When Edgar neared the bridge, the two dogs took off after him, barking madly. They drove him right off the road.

The motorcycle skidded off the road. Fortunately the basket and the cats bounced out of the sidecar and landed safely on the river bank, for the dogs chased Edgar across the river and up under the arch of the bridge. Thoroughly shaken, Edgar drove off without looking back.

The cats were unharmed, but when
they woke up the next morning, they
were terrified.

"Where are we?" meowed the kittens.
Before Duchess could reassure them,
an alley cat jumped out in front of them.

"O'Malley at your service!" he said. "Is
there anything I can do to help?"

"We are lost," explained Duchess. She told him their story. "I know how to get to Paris," he said with a smile.

O'Malley went to the road. A milk truck drove by and he leaped onto the hood, startling the driver to a full stop. Then he ushered everyone on board.

"This is great!" cried Berlioz, who was hungry. "Look at all this milk!"

The milkman started up his truck and drove away. But when he glanced in his rearview mirror, he saw five cats lapping up his milk. He pulled off to the side of the road.

"Get out, you beasts!" he cried, furious.

O'Malley and the Aristocats jumped out and ran as fast as they could.

O'Malley came up with another idea.
"Let's follow the railway tracks back to
Paris," he suggested. The kittens took the
lead, whistling as they went along.

While they were crossing the bridge, a train appeared. O'Malley quickly pushed everyone onto the trestle below. They huddled together as the train thundered by above them. But Marie, terrified, slipped off the bridge into the river below. O'Malley jumped after her at once. He swam over to the little kitten and brought her back to shore safely.

Duchess looked on, amazed and grateful. "He may be an alley cat," she thought, "but he is very brave and strong!"

When O'Malley reached the shore, she thanked him for saving her daughter's life.

O'Malley and the Aristocats walked all day. Finally, in the evening, they reached Paris. O'Malley led them up to the rooftops. Little Marie was very tired.

"Come on! I'll carry you," offered O'Malley. Marie was delighted.

"This is fun!" cried Berlioz, enjoying the adventure.

"Yeah, I love it!" seconded Toulouse. "Look at the view!"

All of a sudden, a lively tune filled the air. It came from an attic a few houses away.

"What's that music?" asked Berlioz, intrigued.

"That's my friend Scat Cat and his band," explained O'Malley. "I can take you to their attic if you like, but let me warn you, Scat's music is not at all like Beethoven's! He plays jazz!"

"May we go?" cried the kittens in unison. They looked over to Duchess for her permission.

"Very well, but you must behave yourselves!" agreed Duchess with a smile. A few minutes later, they were all peering in through Scat Cat's skylight.

"I'd like to introduce you to my friend Scat Cat," said O'Malley with a grin.

Scat Cat was stretched out on his bed holding his trumpet. A Siamese cat was playing the piano and an Italian cat was playing the concertina. There was a guitarist and a drum player, too. They welcomed Duchess and her kittens with a jazzy tune.

Then Scat Cat played a solo for Duchess, who was very touched. She offered to play the harp in return.

O'Malley sat at her feet and gazed at her lovingly. One of the cats joined her on the bass. The beautiful sound of the harp filled the room, and Duchess received a hearty round of applause at the end.

Everyone played and danced until the wee hours of the morning. Scat Cat and his band went on their way and, after promising that they would soon come back, O'Malley, Duchess and the kittens went out on the roofs. Duchess and O'Malley sat together on a chimney and gazed at the starry night.

"I like O'Malley," announced Berlioz, suppressing a yawn.

"I do too," agreed Toulouse. "He's so nice!"

"I think Mother likes him too," said Marie, smiling. "I hope he stays with us!"

Duchess did like O'Malley very much. She was very grateful for everything he had done for them.

The following morning, O'Malley brought the Aristocats to Madame Bonfamille's house. Berlioz, Toulouse, and Marie ran ahead to the front door. They couldn't wait to see Madame and be back home. Duchess lingered behind.

"Thank you, O'Malley," she said. "You've been very kind to us and I'll never forget you."

"Good-bye and good luck," said O'Malley at the front door.
"If I can ever help you again, just call on me, okay?"
Duchess nodded. She was sad to see him go.

Berlioz, Toulouse, and Marie were impatiently scratching at the front door. It was abruptly opened, but not by Madame. Edgar, looking very surprised, stood in the doorway. O'Malley quickly slipped away.

As soon as the cats were
in the hallway, Edgar
caught them in a bag.
Duchess, Toulouse, Berlioz,
and Marie meowed and
scratched, but Edgar
wouldn't let them go.
Roquefort, who had come
to welcome his friends, was
horrified.

He watched Edgar hide the cats in the
oven, and swore he would find help for
his friends.

Roquefort left the house in search O'Malley. When he found him, he explained what had happened. O'Malley sent him looking for Scat Cat and his friends.

Roquefort was nervous. He didn't like cats much—the Aristocats were an exception—and he knew cats didn't like him either. But the Aristocats' lives were at stake, and Roquefort bravely approached Scat Cat and his band. They picked him up by his tail and began to tease him.

"Your friend O'Malley sent me!" squeaked Roquefort, desperate. "Duchess and the kittens are in danger! O'Malley needs your help!"

At once, the cats let him go. Roquefort quickly told them what had happened. "Show us the way!" ordered Scat Cat.

Meanwhile, in the stables, Edgar had put the cats in a trunk addressed to Timbuktu. O'Malley tried to stop him, but Edgar pinned him to the wall with a pitchfork.

Scat Cat and his friends jumped on Edgar, meowing and scratching madly. Soon the butler was pinned to the floor. Scat Cat freed O'Malley while Roquefort unlocked the trunk. Duchess and the kittens emerged, relieved.

Frou-Frou, Madame's horse, was eager to get into the action too. With one swift kick, she sent Edgar reeling into the trunk as everyone cheered.

The movers came to pick up the trunk. "I wonder why they want this heavy trunk sent to Timbuktu," sighed one of them. "It's so far away!" The cats giggled, hiding in the stables.

Scat Cat and his band left, but not before Duchess and the kittens had thanked them and promised to visit soon. O'Malley stayed. He did not want to leave until Duchess, the kittens, and Madame were reunited. The old lady was very relieved and happy that her cats were safe and sound. To everyone's delight, she asked O'Malley to stay and join her family.

O'Malley did stay and what a handsome family they made! Madame took a wonderful photograph for the family album.

The Wonderful World of Disney